DOOGIE DORK'S WISH

By

Mavis Tofte

CREATIVE QUILL

Library of Congress Control Number:2002096717

ISBN: 0-9709906-2-6

First Edition 2003

All art work and illustrations by Mavis Tofte

Cascade Printing Company . Salem, OR

Doogie Dork's Wish

Part I

Long ago and not so far away a family
of Dorks lived in the land beyond imagination

and not far from the truth. It was a wonderful place where the ruling elders were wise and the land provided for all their needs. The Dorks were bright, intelligent, hard working, and kind. Many were known as "oodle noodles" because they were so intelligent. They loved the natural beauty of their homeland, including the flowers, the animals, and all growing things. In other words, Dorks were just the opposite of what they referred to as a "gluck". Everyone who is anyone knows that a "gluck" is a person who is odd and doesn't fit in.

Dorkland is where Doogie Dork lived with his mother, father, brothers, sisters, aunts, uncles, and his good friend, Finnegan. Doogie and Finnegan attended school through the winter. Doogie loved to study about other countries and dreamed of the time when he could visit one of them. It was his favorite subject. He didn't like noisy places with crowded cities, over-sized shopping malls, and factories. Young Doogie was fascinated with a quaint tourist attraction that was nestled in a forest found in the State of Oregon. He saw pictures of visitors with their children enjoying the park and according to their smiling faces; they seemed to be having such a wonderful time. It looked "meech", Dork talk meaning very special. He whispered to Finnegan about his wish to someday visit the beautiful Enchanted

Forest. It was all he could think about. If only he could!

One day, the Grand Elder came to school to make a special announcement about the coming summer, after school was out. During the next two weeks there was going to be a contest to grant one wish to the young Dork who worked the hardest to follow the Dork rules of behavior. The winner would be given a choice of either a special gift or a trip to visit a land outside of Dorkville. The length of the visit could be for a few days or for the summer depending on the winner's ability to follow Dork visiting rules. Doogies eyes lit up and he slapped Finnegan on the back for joy. This was his chance! No one would see a Dork work as hard as he would. Doogie thought he had wished so much to visit the Enchanted Forest that the elders must have noticed. At least it seemed that way.

Doogie burst with energy. His short legs turned into little tornados moving him swiftly as he went about the task in front of him. However, other young Dorks would do their best too. Dorkville became a beehive of activity. Young Dorks scampered everywhere. The elders just smiled as they watched. Doogie became a regular "gubb", meaning hard worker in Dorkland. Doogie carried wood for his father, weeded the garden, carried the groceries for his mother, picked up his clothes and cleaned his room. He helped his family without being asked. But would it be enough? What could he do to give him the edge? His friends were also trying very hard. Doogie was worried.

He was sure Buffo Dork was ahead on points and time was running out. Because Buffo was big and strong, he could do so much more than the others. He could carry more wood, tote more groceries, and watch more children. The big Dork was also a "gubb". Buffo wanted to win so he could go on a cruise for the summer. He loved ships. This was why he tried so hard. If Doogie lost, he would have to wait until he was bigger and stronger. But that time seemed so far away. The little Dork was more determined than ever and he would give it his very best effort. This was the last day but he had one more chance to get a lot of points which might put him over the top. Doogie would really have to hurry now and he ran faster than ever.

The young Dork was on his way to the fire station where he would be allowed to clean the big fire engine. He was supposed to go there straight from school and the job would take him the rest of the day. The sooner he got there the more he could do. He was hurrying as fast as his short legs could go. On his way from school Doogie heard a strange noise, sort of a yelp or the sound of something hurt. What was that?

Then he heard the sound again but it seemed weaker. If he stopped to check it out, Doogie might lose his big chance to win. But the helpless yelp sounded so sad that the little Dork knew he must help if he could. He turned toward the sound and soon came upon a well. He looked over the edge and discovered that a puppy had fallen in and was now struggling for his very life.

Doogie didn't hesitate and began to lower the well bucket so the puppy could get in. The puppy was so weak that it took all his remaining strength to get into the bucket. Then the young Dork pulled as hard as he could to raise the bucket with the puppy to the top. Soon he could see the little dog's wet nose poke over the edge of the bucket. Whew! That was a "coti" meaning close call in Dork talk.

Doogie hugged the little dog and held him close so the puppy knew that everything would be all right and that he was safe. The little Dork softly whispered, "sokay", "sokay" "little one". Of course this was Dork talk meaning everything was all right. The puppy licked his face and showered him with thankful puppy kisses.

The owners had been looking for the missing dog and came running when they saw the two of them. The wet puppy was returned to its grateful owners. It made Doogie feel good to see them so happy. He sighed sadly because it was too late to help at the fire station and by now Buffo was probably there to help out. It seemed almost impossible for the little Dork to get his wish by winning the contest. Time had run out. But it was late and he must go home so his own family wouldn't worry.

The next day, everyone gathered at the town square to hear what the elders had to say. Buffo was smiling and confidant for he had worked very hard and he was about to receive his reward. Finnegan patted Doogie on the shoulder as they watched together. The elders praised all the young Dorks for trying their very best and each was given a medal for their efforts. It was decided to have a picnic to celebrate the event before the grand prize winner was announced. Doogie and Finnegan had a lot of fun playing games and eating good food at the picnic. They especially loved a tasty Dorkland treat called "Yum-Yums". Even though he wouldn't win the grand prize, everything was very "zooky" meaning cool in Dork talk. It was turning out to be a pretty good day after all.

The elders soon arrived and all eyes turned in their direction. In Dorkland, all elders were treated with respect because they were very wise and intelligent "oodle noo-dles". Everyone listened to the elders. Doogie watched the excitement grow on Buffo's face and the little Dork thought about how much fun his friend would have this summer. After all it was a good contest and everyone had their chance to win. The elders began to whisper among themselves before making their announcement. What in the world could be the problem? The elders nodded their heads in agreement and turned to face the eager contestants. They approached clos-er.

Then the elders raised their hands as they motioned for all to be quiet. A hush grew over the crowd. Doogie looked at Buffo and knew that whatever happened now, his oversized friend had earned his reward. He must be congratulated for his good fortune. The Grand Elder began to speak and told about all the points that Buffo had earned and he would be rewarded for his efforts.

"However", he paused briefly, "we have among us a "meech" (Dork talk meaning someone very special). One of you gave up a chance to win the most points by helping to save an unfortunate puppy that might have drowned if left alone in the water".

The Grand Elder slowly looked around at the young Dork faces as they waited eagerly for his words. "For this unselfish act, **Doogie Dork** will receive a special grand prize and his wish will be granted", continued the Grand Elder as he looked at Doogie. "Even though your wish to visit the

Enchanted Forest for the summer will be granted; there are conditions that you must meet in order to spend the whole summer. You will be given a time limit to fulfill the Dork rules for travelers. If you fail, you can not stay and will be whisked back to Dorkville immediately. You must prove yourself to be a worthy representative of all Dorks. The Dork rules say that you must blend into your new surroundings and make yourself useful."

The elders cautioned Doogie that this might be harder than it sounded. After all he was still very young and had a lot to learn. They shook his hand and wished him well. The Grand Elder solemnly spoke to the little Dork who was told that when he was ready; Doogie would wear the magic hat that could take him to his destination in the twinkling of an eye. All he would have to do is close his eyes and repeat the magic words three times. The official Dork hat would take him there and return him when the time would be right.

Doogie was so excited that he could hardly stand still. His feet wanted to dance a jig. He said goodbye to his family, Finnegan, and Buffo. The elders smiled and nodded their heads as they wished him well. He was told that when his time was up and he returned, he could share the story of his adventure with the rest of them.

The Grand Elder placed the magical Dork hat on his head and Doogie was told to close his eyes. They turned him around slowly as he spoke the precious words, "I wish I were there, I wish I were there, I wish I were there". A gentle wind blew around him and lifted him like a leaf in the breeze. The Dork voices faded as he spun away from them. Then he felt something solid under his feet and Doogie slowly opened his eyes.

Part Two

Oh, my! He was standing by a bush near a castle just like the one in the picture he had seen in a travel book. The little Dork rubbed his eyes in disbelief. He had arrived at the Enchanted Forest just like the elders said he would. How lucky could a Dork be! This was the place he had dreamed about. It was really "lux", Dork talk meaning quality or grand. Uh, oh, other people were arriving and he had better be about his business. Now what was it that the elders had said he must do in order to stay for the summer? They said that he must follow the Dork rules of behavior with only three days to blend in and make himself useful. He looked around and noted that a sign said "Start at the Castle". O.K., that's where Doogie would begin his new adventure. He turned toward the Castle and started his journey.

The little Dork's heart beat for joy! This beautiful forest park was beyond his wildest dreams. Wow! This was lux! As he looked around he was having trouble containing his joy and tending to the task at hand. Just think here he was a lowly little Dork in this magnificent forest and he had a chance to spend the rest of the summer. If only he could find out where he belonged in order to be useful and blend into his surroundings. Then he quickly started down the brick path on the other side of the Castle. The little Dork had no idea what troubles lay ahead to get in the way of his good intentions.

As he followed the trail on the other side of the Castle, Doogie spotted a gingerbread house that looked good enough to eat. There was a sign in front that said "**HANSEL AND GRETEL**". Now our young Dork was about to learn a valuable lesson. This pink frosting coated house looked so inviting that he thought maybe he could stay here to be useful.

He looked in the dark doorway and was horrified by what he saw. On the inside an old witch smiled, beckoning him to come in and have something to eat with her. She already had Hansel and Gretel under her spell and was trying to trick Gretel into the oven. "Oh, my, maybe she wanted him for lunch too", thought Doogie.

It was too much, Doogie felt as if his hair were standing on end. This was not a good idea. If he tried to fit in here, he might end up on the witch's dinner plate. This fitting in rule was going to take longer than he thought. The little Dork slowly backed away because he didn't want to make the witch angry. Then he ran as fast as his short legs could go!

He looked back at the gingerbread house which still looked tasty and reminded him that he was getting hungry. Being a clever Dork he would plan on eating at some other place. One last parting glance brought to mind the old saying; "All that glitters is not gold!" Well, that's one lesson he would remember.

Although Humpty-Dumpty was an egg, he was not for eating. The Mad Hatter was serving tea, a spider was watching Miss Muffet as she ate her breakfast, while Jack and Jill had spilled their bucket of water. Even the tea the Mad Hatter was serving was only pretend. None of these seemed too appealing to a hungry Dork. Further ahead, Doogie heard the sweet voice of someone singing. As he rounded the corner, he saw an inviting stone cottage with a thatched roof.

Now this looked more like something for him. Snow White was the person singing in the cottage as she swept the floor. When he peeked in the window, she invited him in for a snack which he accepted. After all that he had been through, Doogie felt sleepy. Snow White noticed how tired he was and invited him to take a nap on one of the beds upstairs.

She lived in this cozy cottage with seven Dwarfs who were working at the mine until quitting time. They would be home later when they finished work for the day. Now this seemed like a great place to stay. He could help them with their work. A tired Doogie soon was fast asleep with visions of happy Dwarfs lulling him to dreamland.

There was singing in the distance as the seven little men were on their way home from work. A tired Doogie slept on. The singing stopped when the little men reached their cottage. But they were a noisy group, like a bunch of children who hadn't learned their manners. Pick axes and tools clattered as they were thrown to the floor. Chair legs scraped as they were dragged out from the table. When Snow White asked them not to make so much noise because they had a guest sleeping upstairs, the Dwarfs immediately rushed up the steps to see the newcomer.

Doogie was startled by the loud racket and sat bolt upright in the bed as the rowdy group approached. Snow White tried to quiet them down so she could introduce everyone. Putting her hand to her mouth, she paused as she said, "Why, I don't believe that I know your name". "Its Doogie", the eager young Dork replied .

One Dwarf, however, was a real grouch and was quick to point out that there weren't enough beds to go around. He said there wasn't room for any more people. He complained about everything. The little Dork began to wonder about him and thought the Dwarf seemed such a "fogel" which in Dork talk means an annoying or bothersome person. The grouchy Dwarf was so rude that he grabbed the blanket where Doogie was resting giving it a sudden jerk. This caused Doogie to go flying and he landed on the floor with a thump. The grouchy Dwarf smiled to himself, hoping that the little Dork would understand that he was not wanted here. The others may be fooled by the Dork's smile, but the grouch wanted nothing to do with him! He wanted to make his feelings very clear to little Doogie.

As he flew through the air, the little Dork had second thoughts about living in this overcrowded cottage. The grouchy Dwarf, who was glad when Doogie decided not to stay, even told him there was a much larger house further up the hill beyond the western town. Snow White and the other Dwarfs were so nice that it was hard to say goodbye. But a few gruff remarks from the grouchy one reminded Doogie why he must move on.

As he continued along the trail, Doogie saw a different house. It wasn't built like most he had seen. It was very crooked. He watched other visitors as they tried to walk through which caused him to laugh as they staggered, trying to reach for the walls. It was fun to watch the people, but he didn't have time to visit. The little Dork had other things on his mind.

Time was passing quickly and young Doogie hadn't fulfilled the Dork rules yet. The little Dork didn't stop at the inviting Shoe Slide because there just wasn't enough time. This situation was getting to be a real "niggle", Dork talk meaning thought provoking problem. He wasn't any closer to his goals than when he started. So, he better move a little faster. Time was running out.

Part Three

Doogie Dork moved as fast as he could and soon came to the western town. He wondered if he could fit in here. The town was small but full of activity and he started to watch some of the children as they tried the different games of skill. Maybe he could play some of the games when he had more time. But for now, the little Dork had to concentrate on the task at hand.

Before he moved on he heard the taunting voice of Johnnie Rio. Doogie listened to what he was saying. The young Dork laughed when he heard the teasing comments of the gunslinger. Johnnie Rio referred to one visitor as a "wall-eyed lizard". He constantly challenged those who passed near enough to hear him. His western talk and colorful comments made Doogie laugh again.

The little Dork decided to walk around the outer edge of the town by strolling along the boardwalk. Soon he started to cross the street, but Doogie didn't watch his step. The young Dork tripped as he stepped off the boardwalk and tumbled into the street, turning head over heels. His antics caused the children to laugh. This made him feel so good that he did other stunts for the children much to the delight of those watching. He acted "blitty", (Dork talk meaning silly or like a clown) to make them laugh even more.

He visited the dentist, the barber, the laundry, and other shop owners. There were, however, no openings for additional help. Well, that was except for the shooting gallery which could use more targets. The sign said, "Job openings, shooting gallery needs fresh targets". That didn't sound too appealing to Doogie. It would probably just bring the undertaker more business. He didn't want to end up under one of the grave markers at Boot Hill. Doogie took a look at some of the tombstones to remind him of some of the reasons why people ended up here. Some of the reasons were strange and even brought a smile to his face.

It did, however, make for some interesting reading.

Fort Fearless already had someone working and there wasn't need for anyone else. The Steering Boats were mechanical and didn't need a live attendant. The elders were right-trying to fit in was not as easy as it sounded. Oh, well! Doogie still had some time to look around but he better move a little faster. What was that place on the other side of the Opera House? He watched as another visitor exited out the other door and he seemed to be fine.

Then Doogie walked through the door that had a sign to the side which said, **"Mc GOON'S SALOON"**. The floor sank and bobbed up and down, making Doggie's short legs feel like rubber. After leaving the saloon, the little Dork staggered and wobbled down the street. He passed near the fort again. Although Fort Fearless looked interesting, unfortunately, there was already a safety worker watching the visitors go down the slide. Doogie began to feel sad. It didn't seem like he was making any progress.

Then he remembered that the grouchy Dwarf had mentioned a big house beyond the western town that probably had plenty of room where he could spend his nights. The little Dork looked about and if he looked carefully he could see part of a house show-ing above the high western town fence. It really was large and would be worth checking out. So he headed in that direction.

Part Four

There it was on the other side of the town. Wow! The gray house looked run down and very old. The windows were broken and the shutters hung at odd angles. Even though it wasn't much for beauty, it did seem to have a lot of room. Doogie marched up the front steps to enter through a dark door. The little Dork hesitated briefly when he heard someone scream inside. He cautiously entered the front hall which was dark and not very inviting. What did they call this place anyway? There was a sign at the start of the walk but he hadn't read it. What was he getting into?

As he passed through the door, the sound of organ music came from a room on the right. The hands playing the organ didn't seem to be attached to anyone. Doogie's hair almost stood on end as a spirited figure at the end of the hall beckoned him to continue. Doogie trembled and swallowed hard as he gathered his courage.

Some other visitors entered and he followed them into the living room. Suddenly, one of the seated figures sprang up, towering over others in the room and seemed to lurch toward them. When this happened one of the visitors screamed causing everyone else to shake in their shoes. Woe is me! It was time to leave the living room. There were some carpeted stairs to one side.

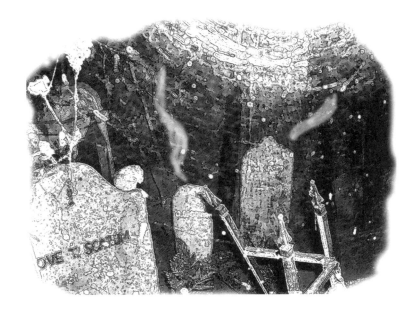

Oh! No! They passed by an eerie graveyard with wispy spooks rising from the grave markers. Doogie was in a "flutz", Dork talk meaning he couldn't make up his mind. The little Dork paused and wondered if he should go forward or turn back. Either way, it was scary. What should he do? He wanted to get out of this place. He scurried to catch up with the group of visitors ahead of him and hoped they would get to the end soon. But there was more to come.

Doors rattled, there were man-eating plants in the arboretum (a room with different types of plants), the bedroom had floating furniture, and ghosts were everywhere. He saw an ever-changing woman's face in the wall, a frightening kitchen with huge rats, and much more. This was a "pud" of a place, Dork talk for messy or disorderly. None of these things seemed like the cozy home Doogie had in mind as a place to spend his nights. He couldn't possibly stay here! He especially had doubts about surviving through a night in this place. The young Dork nervously asked one of the other visitors, "What kind of house is this place?" The reply came as no surprise, "It's a Haunted House, of course". Doogie gasped as he realized the nasty trick that the grouchy Dwarf had pulled on him. He definitely would not fit in here and didn't want to.

He soon was startled by a hideous, grinning skull in an upstairs wall. The flickering candle light did not add too her charm. One of the visitors said that many years ago she used to be a Beauty Queen. The little Dork found this hard to believe as he stared at the shock of dark hair falling across her forehead. How could this be true? He shuddered as the group of visitors moved deeper into the spooky interior of the haunted halls.

Their group finally passed a pair of
singing skeletons on the way to the exit tun-
nel. The young Dork's knees trembled, his
heart beat faster, his hair seemed to be
standing on end, and he shook as his soul
was gripped with fear. Little Doogies stubby
legs moved faster and faster as he quickly

darted from the Haunted House exit. He was so frightened that he dashed back through the western town street not stopping along the way.

He sped past Fort Fearless, the Indian Caves, and only glanced at the snow capped peaks of Ice Mountain. His little legs began to slow down as he turned the corner and headed up a wide stone path. Doogie finally stopped to catch his breath. He was really feeling "wampy", meaning very tired or exhausted in Dork talk. He looked around to see where he was. A huge wooden structure loomed ahead of him. It seemed to be open on one side. The little Dork moved closer to check it out and see what the other people were doing there. Could it be a shelter of some sort where he could sit down and rest?

Part Five

By now, Doogie was very "wampy". He had done a lot of walking, entertaining the children in the western town, and the Haunted House visit; all had left him out of breath. If only he could sit down and rest under the trees for a while. That large building ahead might be just the place to catch his breath. The little Dork waited for some people who were approaching behind him. He let them pass and followed them up the steps. Then he watched to see what they were going to do.

To one side he saw what looked like a peaceful stream going up the mountain. "Oh, look", the young Dork exclaimed. There were logs floating on the stream. They were hollowed out and people were sitting in them, enjoying a relaxing ride up the mountain. Doogie looked up and saw a large sign on the outside of the building. The words spelled out the letters, **"BIG TIMBER Log Ride"**. Wonderful, just what he needed was a nice restful log ride on a quiet mountain stream. The little Dork noticed that some visitors wore ponchos or large plastic bags over their clothes. He thought that was a little strange and wondered why.

Oh, well! Doogie decided that he would take a ride in the log too and relax while he thought about what to do next. An attendant helped him settle into a waiting log. This was going to be fun, the little Dork thought. He thanked the young man who had assisted him. Then the log began to move slowly up the mountain. Doogie leaned back and thought to himself that this was the life! It was very lux. No worries now. All he had to do was sit back and relax.

He was really enjoying the ride as the log began to pass through an old logging mill with some animated loggers at work. Doogie had a little time to think and he remembered that someone had mentioned there might be a possibility of spending the night with an elderly woodcarver who lived in the Old World Village. The friendly old man's name was Geppetto. He had carved a puppet that later became a real live boy. What a nice thought. Doogie relaxed and was enjoying the ride now that he had a plan of what he should do after his ride.

Suddenly, the log lurched forward and dropped down following a sharp dip in the track. The little Dork gasped. What happened? Wow! Someone must have made a mistake in the design. Doogie barely had time to gather his thoughts when the log began to slowly climb again going higher and higher. Then the log seemed to pause as it teetered at the peek of the climb. The young Dork's eyes opened wide when he saw what lay ahead. "Oh, no. Help!", thought the little Dork. They suddenly plunged straight down the mountain for what seemed like an eternity to Doogie. He was terrified. What was a Dork to do? Was this going to be the end of his short life? Was he going to survive?

As the log hit the pond at the bottom, a huge spray of water covered him which explained why he had seen some people earlier wearing rain slickers. The log slowed down and drifted toward the unloading dock, much to Doogies relief. It was not the end of the world after all, but that was enough excitement for one day, at least for this young Dork. He got out of the log at the dock and smiled weakly at those around him. He staggered away on his wobbly legs. Once again, the young Dork learned that things were not always what they first seemed. He looked himself over to be sure that everything was in one piece and not bits of him all over the place.

He had enough of the log ride at least for now. Doogie started down the brick path heading toward Ice Mountain. That was the way for him to go to find Geppetto who lived in the Old World Village. When he got to the mountain, he could get better directions to the Old World Village. He hoped his luck would be better this time when he met Geppetto and Pinocchio. He could hardly wait to find them!

Part Six

Doogie asked other visitors which way to go to get to the Old World Village. He was told that it wasn't far, just the other side of Ice Mountain. As he passed Ice Mountain, the little Dork thought it would be fun to go on the bob sleds when he had more time. At least he was hoping to have more time. If only he could find something special for him to do at the Enchanted Forest.

He wanted to find the old woodcarver whose name was Geppetto to see if he was as friendly as people had said. The little Dork heard that the carver had made a special wooden puppet that later turned into a real boy. Maybe Doogie could play with him. As the young Dork strolled through the village, he was tempted by the many sights. He stopped briefly to read the notices that were posted on a bulletin board to see if anything applied to his needs. It was fun to read but he better move on since none of the notices needed his help.

There was Pinocchio's Playroom, the Gravity Factory, and the Blackbird Bakery among the many things to see. As he approached the Blackbird Bakery, the little Dork saw that Geppetto's shop was just across the street. What luck! Geppetto was at home.

The old man invited Doogie into his shop. He was so friendly that the little Dork immediately liked him. Geppetto introduced the young Dork to Pinocchio and told him the story of how the puppet became a real boy. Geppetto said that Doogie could spend all his nights with them as long as he was visiting the Enchanted Forest. Pinocchio could use some company and they had plenty of room.

Doogie knew that he had only one more day to fulfill the Dork rules in order to spend the whole summer here. He had a lot of ground to cover. His summer, his wish, and all his dreams were on the line. It would be up to him to make it happen. There was so much to do and he hadn't even seen the beautiful Fantasy Fountains. He could only remember the pictures that he had seen at school.

He went to bed knowing that he faced a real "dongle". This is a Dork word meaning puzzling task. Doogie fell into a deep sleep, dreaming of what might be.

The little Dork woke early to the smell of breakfast cooking. After eating, Geppetto and Pinocchio wished him luck and shook his hand. Then Doogie started out on his last day to try to fulfill the Dork rules. "If all goes well, we'll see you tonight" were their parting words. Doogie waved as he started on his way. It would be his last chance to spend the rest of the summer here. With a wistful sigh the little Dork thought to himself, if only he could find a way to make it happen.

Part Seven

Doogie began his final search to find where he could be useful and fit in. He looked here and he looked there. The young Dork would leave no stone unturned to find where he was needed. If only someone would give him a chance. The right opportunity was all he needed. He didn't know which way to turn, or where he should look next. He was in a "flutz", Dorkland talk for not knowing which way to turn. His short legs carried him up and down the mountain. But, so far, he couldn't find the answer to his problem.

The little Dork hurried as fast as he could and was actually wending his way higher and higher. By now he was so worn out that he needed to find a place to sit down. He knew better than to rest at Big Timber log ride and hastily moved past it. Doogie wandered up a path that led to the Fairweather Theater where there were benches for the visitors. Since it was between shows, the benches were empty. It was a perfect place for him to sit for a short time.

The exhausted Dork sat down on one of the wooden benches. He put his chin in his hands and gave a great sigh. What was he to do now? The time limit was almost over and he hadn't found a way to be useful so he could fit in and stay for the rest of the summer. Doogie wanted so much to spend his vacation here! He loved watching the visitors, especially the children. Hearing the laughter of children made him tingle all over. He was already making friends, but if something didn't happen soon, the magic hat would surely whisk him away. The Dork elders, his family, and friends at Dorkland would be so disappointed in him.

Children and their parents began to arrive for the next scheduled show. There was a lot of chattering going on as the crowd grew. But wait, something was wrong! One of the actors stepped onto the stage to make an announcement. There would be a delay in starting the next show because one of the actors had an accident and could not go on. If they couldn't find a replacement, the show would be cancelled.

What they needed was a Dork for the play. It should be noted that the play that year was "Snow White and the Seven Dorks". The injured actor was one of the Dorks. They couldn't go on unless another Dork was found quickly. Doogie almost jumped out of his skin and the little Dork wondered, "Did his ears deceive him? Did he hear right or was it just wishful thinking? Were they really in need of another Dork? It was true! Hallelujah!" This was definitely going to be "Zooky", Dork talk meaning cool, a happy feeling.

Doogie eagerly ran up to the Director who was in charge of the play. The little Dork pleaded, "Please give me a chance. I'm a Dork and I love to make children laugh!" The Director took him aside and explained the things that he would have to do. "Oh, yes, yes! Please give me a chance; I'm perfect for the part. I am available right away and can work for the whole summer. You won't be disappointed," the little Dork pleaded.

The worried director paused deep in thought and then a smile slowly spread across her face. "You certainly look like a Dork and we do need one right now. All right, you can fill in for the day. Then, if you do a good job, you can work for the rest of the summer" she stated. Doogie smiled and thought "Oh, boy! This was great"! It was such a "coti", Dork talk meaning close call. He almost felt the magic hat start to tingle and tighten on his head when time seemed to be running out. But as soon as arrangements were made the magic hat felt normal again.

Doogie tossed his hat in the air for joy. "You won't be disappointed" he said as they both walked backstage to the dressing room. The Director gave him his last minute instructions. "Wow", thought the little Dork, "this was great"!

Then one of the actors stepped onto the stage from behind the curtain and made an announcement that the play would go on as scheduled. They had found a replacement. The anxious audience clapped their hands and cheered at the news. The crowd grew still as the curtain began to open and the play was under way.

The little Dork fit right in. He beamed a grateful smile as he was accepted by the actors and an appreciative audience. After the play, his heart warmed as he was welcomed by all. This was better than he had ever hoped.

After the show, the cast gathered in front to say good-bye to the audience. Some of the parents brought their children closer so they could talk to the actors. Doogie Dork beamed because he was now part of that select group.

He could hardly wait to tell Geppetto and Pinocchio the good news. So much had happened to him on this very special day. Doogie would be able to spend the rest of the summer at the Enchanted Forest. There were so many things to tell his new friend Pinocchio.

Part Eight

Doogies summer turned out to be so "Zooky", Dork talk meaning cool or a lot of fun. He turned out to be a very good visitor from Dorkland. The little Dork had found a place to be useful where he was really needed and he could certainly blend into a play about Dorks. Between plays he could visit other places at the Enchanted Forest. He especially loved to visit the Jolly Roger where he could watch the dramatic, colorful water show called "Fantasy Fountains". The music guided him through the story of the ever changing waters. It was a "ringo", meaning a real winner in Dork talk.

Doogie felt like one of the luckiest Dorks in the world. His new friends, his dream summer, everything was so "meech", a word meaning very special in Dork talk. The young Dork enjoyed picnicing under the trees and eating delicious ice cream cones. That was a delicacy not found at Dorkland.

When he returned, there would be so much to tell everyone at Dorkland. The young Dork could tell his friend Finnegan about staying with Geppetto and Pinocchio. Geppetto sure made good pancakes! They were delicious. He used a special mix called Han's Heavenly Pancake Mix. Not only would he tell them of his adventure but Doogie could also find out about Buffo and his experience on his cruise vacation. When the time came to go home, it would be sad to leave his new friends. It would, however, be great to see his family and friends at Dorkland. It would, especially, be so nice to see his home again.

Perhaps, one last look at "kiddyland", for memories sake and then it would be time to go.

The time had come. He closed his eyes and felt the magic hat grip tighter on his head. Then he repeated three times the magic words, "I wish I were there, I wish I were there, I wish I were there". He felt wind swirling around him as he spun in space. Soon he felt the ground under his feet. Doogie opened his eyes and smiled from ear to ear. There was his family, Finnegan, Buffo, and the people of Dorkland. He hugged everyone in his family. Somewhere in the background he saw the the little puppy that he had saved. It's fun to visit other places but this was home. Dorkland and everything in it looked so wonderful! Doogie now knew that visiting other places was fun, but nothing could take the place of home.

All the people of Dorkland gathered at the town square where the two travelers could tell of their adventures and of the people they met. They could also tell of the many new things they had learned about.

Buffo told about the ship he had traveled on. He told about the delicious food, the swimming pool, and the games for the guests. He helped in the kitchen and was told that he had a natural talent as a Chef. One look at Buffo and everyone nodded their heads in agreement.

Now it was Doogies turn to tell what had happened to him. He told them about the beautiful and lux Enchanted Forest nestled in the woods with its colorful fountains, fairyland trail, western town, and the dreaded Haunted House. The little Dork laughed when he told them about the Log Ride where he thought he was going to relax. He proudly told them that he worked in a summer play about "Snow White and the Seven Dorks". There was so much to tell, but he must not forget to mention his new friends like the Director, Geppetto, Snow White, and Pinocchio and many others. Doogie told them about ice cream cones and the fine pancakes that Geppetto made. He thanked them for his trip and hugged everyone again because it was good to be home, too!

DORK TALK

More *DORK TALK*